THE REAL
CHOCOLATE RABBIT

Jaymee Jean Willison

Photos from pixabay:
 Fawn - rottonara
 Bear - thepoorphotographer
 Coyote - skeeze
 Owl - digidreamgrafix
 Dwarf rabbit - Hans
 Bus - intiawka_vg

Modified by Jaymee Willison

All other photographs taken by and modified by Jaymee Willison

ebooklaunch.com took the concept and photos I had for the cover and made it into one.

Scribendi Editors EM328 and EM1438 Edited and proofread the book. Thank you.

Formatting by Polgarus Studio. Thank you.

Thank you Teri Willison for triple checking I not only got all the family's names in but spelled them correctly.

How could I ever thank Kristy Dial and Sheri Ruben for the countless hours of help they gave me? Never could!!

Thank you!

This book is dedicated to Art

Wish you were here

Chapter 1

"We won! We won! Mom, Dad, Jaymee, we won!"

Artie dropped his backpack inside the door and raced around the house. He ran from room to room until he found his mom, his dad, and his sister Jaymee, who were all gathered in the kitchen.

"Slow down, Artie. You won what? What is this all about?" his mom Berita asked.

"Our class, Mom. We won the contest! It's a trip. We get to go to the chocolate factory. We get to take a tour. Mommmm, remember? I told you—the science class contest. I talked to you about it a long time ago. Well, we found out today that we won, so our whole class gets to go on a tour of the chocolate factory." Artie was so excited the words were spilling out of his mouth almost before he could think of them. "You know Mom, they don't usually do tours." He stopped talking for a second to take a breath.

Jaymee jumped in and said, "It's because of safety and sanitation reasons. That's why they never give any tours. I remember hearing that at school last year. I always thought it would be so cool to see how chocolate bunnies and hollow eggs are made. I never thought I would know anyone who got to go on a tour!" Jaymee squealed a tiny bit, as she was so excited for Artie.

"Dad, I told you about the contest too, remember?" Artie said.

"Well, I can't honestly say as I do remember," Artie's dad Harley answered.

"Gee, Dad, the only reason they are letting our class go on this tour is because the chocolate company is introducing a new chocolate character this year. It's a humongous secret, though, exactly what it is. As part of the unveiling, they're allowing one class tour. So we had a contest at school to see which class got to go. Well, today we found out our science class won! Our whole class gets to go on the tour.

"We will all learn how the chocolate pieces are made; you know, the eggs, the coins, and lots of other things! Oh yes, and the chocolate bunnies. Then, of course, they will tell us all about their new character.

Maybe it's a chicken or a duck, who knows? Whatever it is, we get to see it first. Must be a super new addition to their collection for them to invite a whole class to go on a tour."

Artie's eyes twinkled as he continued. "Anyway, it's perfect that our science class won. We'll discover how they melt the chocolate in big huge pots, and we'll get to watch as it's poured into different molds and how they do something called 'tempering the chocolate.' That's the real science part! I don't know what tempering is or what it does, but I will know soon. Oh, it will be great! Hip, hip, hooray!"

Jaymee got so caught up in Artie's excitement she grabbed his hand, and they both started being silly, swirling around the kitchen together with Jaymee's long brown pigtails flying in the air.

Artie stopped swirling and said, "Oh, I can't wait. I love chocolate bunnies, or rabbits, whatever they are. Are they bunnies or rabbits? I wonder . . .hmm . . . bunny rabbits, maybe?"

"That is great," his mom said. Then she asked, "When is it? When is this tour?"

Artie answered, "It's in two weeks, Mom. On Friday."

"Oh my goodness, Artie. That's the day you and Jaymee are flying to Minden to see your Grandpa Art and Nana Jean. Honey, we have to be at the airport Friday afternoon. Darn it, Artie. I hate to say this and spoil everything, but I don't think you are going to be able to go on that school outing."

Harley looked at his wife, and then at Artie and Jaymee, as he said, "That would be terrible for Artie to miss this opportunity. We'll have to sit down and do some thinking on the timing and see what we can do." He glanced back and winked at both the kids.

Berita saw the wink and lifted her eyebrow at him. She gave her husband that mother's stare, the one usually saved for the kids. "Now, dear, let's not get his hopes up until we see if the timing is going to work," she said.

"Oh gosh, Mom," Artie said. "It will be okay. The tour will be over and we will be back at school by eleven o'clock, and absolutely no later than eleven-thirty, because that's when school is out for spring break."

"Well, Artie, we'll have to see."

"Noooooooo!" Artie protested. "Mom, I have to go. This is really important. We can do both, Mom, really.

Daaaaad, tell Mom it's okay, will ya?"

"I think he is right, Berita," Harley said. "It won't be a problem getting them to the plane. There will be enough time. Even if they are a little late, the traffic will be light. I figure we'll get them there. Maybe even early."

Berita waved her hands in the air to show she was giving up and said, "Well, okay. If you think so."

Harley smiled at both the kids and gave them the thumbs up.

"Yay, yay!" Both Artie and Jaymee shouted with joy then jumped around the kitchen.

Jaymee was so happy for Artie because she knew how he loved finding out what makes things work and how things are made—the hows, whys, and wherefores in the world. She loved that about him, always wanting all the answers.

Chapter 2

Two weeks later, first thing in the morning, Jaymee went to Artie's room. He was sitting on his bed, looking like he was thinking very deeply about something. "Oh boy, Artie," she said. "Today's the big day. Aren't you just so-o-o-o excited?"

Artie didn't say a word.

"Artie . . . hello," Jaymee called out. "Hello in there. Aren't you excited?" She was just a bit worried now.

"Oh . . ." Artie looked up at her. "Oh, yes, Jaymee, I'm very excited. I can hardly wait to see Grandpa Art and Grandma Jean, the airplane ride, their new place in Minden, everything. Just going to Nevada is exciting—cowboys, Indians, Wild West land, just like in the movies. Maybe we will even be able to see a real cow or a horse."

"No, silly, I know all that," Jaymee said. "I mean excited about the chocolate factory tour."

"Oh yeah, that too, Jaymee. It's just . . ."

"What? What is it, Artie?" Jaymee walked over and sat down next to him on the bed.

"Well, yes, I'm excited about the tour, but I just wish . . . Well, I just wish we had enough money to buy a nice present for Grandpa and Nana. If we could take them a chocolate bunny or a beautiful egg, that would be great, especially since it is almost Easter. They always send us such a nice, big Easter basket. I wish we could give them something for once." He sighed and folded his hands together. "I already know what you're going to say, Jaymee. With Dad being out of work, we don't have any money, so we can't buy anything. I just really *wish* we could."

Jaymee smiled. There was a little sparkle in her eyes as she reached over and ruffled his sandy blond hair. "Well, Artie, you never know," she said. "Sometimes wishes do come true. I wasn't going to tell you this right now, but I guess I will, just to cheer you up a little. I have three dollars saved up from babysitting. Mom and Dad said I could keep it for our trip. You can take it, Artie, and maybe buy a little something for Grandpa and Nana at the factory after the tour today.

"The chocolate factory might sell items, and you

could get a small bunny, an egg, or even some gold-wrapped coins. I want you to have the money and buy something. We'll take it to them from both of us. It doesn't have to be much, but it will still make them very happy."

"Oh boy!" Artie said. "Do you think I'll be able to find something for them? That is so great of you, Jaymee! Thank you." Artie got up and did a little twirl.

"Well, I hope you can get something." Jaymee said.

 "I think it's a terrific idea. I know Grandpa and Nana have been sending Mom and Dad money from time to time, and they bought our plane tickets. I know they don't have a whole lot of money for extras right now either, but they sure do what they can to help all of us. It would be fantastic to do something special for them."

"Jaymee," Artie said softly, "do you think we are going to be homeless?"

"Golly, I sure hope not, Artie," Jaymee sighed. "I really don't think so. I know Dad is looking everywhere for a job. I am sure he'll find one soon. I have been praying, and knowing you as well as I do, I know you have been praying every day too."

"Well," Artie said, "I know we have to have faith. I guess we just don't know what's going to happen." He lowered his voice to almost a whisper. "Sometimes, at night, I hear Mom crying. I even hear Dad crying now and then. That's when I get scared, and I feel like crying too." Artie looked at Jaymee and wiped away the hint of tears starting to well up in his eyes. "Do you think that's why we are going to Grandpa's for a while? Because Mom and Dad need a little time without us here to talk and try to figure things out? Do you think that's why, Jaymee?"

He sat back down on the bed next to Jaymee. "I know we have to hold on and have faith, Jaymee. I believe it. I know somehow it will be okay. That's the one and only thing I know for sure. I just don't know when or how. That's what makes it so hard."

"You're right, Artie. It will be okay. Mom and Dad will tell us what's going on when we need to know. Right now, we'll keep saying our prayers. That's the best thing we can do for all of us."

Jaymee took the three dollars from her pocket and put them into Artie's little hand. Leaning over, she gave her little brother a big hug.

"Wow, Jaymee!" Artie shouted. "I have a dollar

fifty. With what both of us have together, I bet we can get something super nice now. A couple of chocolate eggs would be good. A chocolate bunny would be the best! Oh, Jaymee, I'm so happy now. What a great surprise for both Nana and Grandpa. Oh boy! Come on! Let's get going!! This tour is going to be so much fun!" He looked over at his sister and added, "Gee, Jaymee, you're the best sister I've ever had."

"Yes, silly. I'm the only sister you've ever had, but thanks, Artie." Jaymee giggled and they both ran downstairs.

Chapter 3

"Come on, kids!" Berita called from the kitchen. "We don't want to be late!"

They all got into the car, buckled up, and off they went.

"Oh, I can hardly wait until we get to the factory," Artie said. "We'll get to see how all the chocolate candies are made. We'll get to see the big chocolate pots, vats, or vessels—I'm not sure what they are called. I know they will be filled to the brim with wonderfully sweet, sweet, thick chocolate. I've always wanted to learn more about the chocolate factory. This is going to be great for our whole science class."

Jaymee was excited too. "Artie, I want to hear about everything. You'll have lots of time to give me all the details while we are on the plane this afternoon. I especially want to hear how they make the chocolate bunnies hollow inside, even though the ears are solid.

The most important thing—the thing that is so cool—is that you get to find out about the new chocolate character. You get to know the biggest secret of all."

Jaymee paused then asked, "Will you be able to talk about the new character after you leave the chocolate factory? Will you be able to tell us what it is? Or will they make you sign something promising never to tell until it comes out to the stores?"

"Gee, Jaymee," Artie said. "I don't know. Good questions. Maybe they will just glue our lips together with thick chocolate so we can never ever talk about it." Artie yanked on Jaymee's sweater and quickly ducked down behind the car seat so she could not yank back.

Artie popped his head back up and asked, "Mom, are you sure you can't come on the tour? They said parents could come."

"No, honey. I have to finish packing for your trip. Your dad has a job interview today and needs the car after I drop Jaymee off at school. The tour sounds like a lot of fun though. We'll be on our way to the airport as soon as it's over. Grandma Jean and Grandpa Art are so excited you're finally coming to visit them. It's been such a long time since they've seen you. I bet they'll be at the airport early to meet you both. They're so excited they might already be there now."

Everyone laughed at that thought.

Berita's heart ached. She missed her mom and dad so much, especially now through all these hard times. Oh, how she wished that she could visit them too. "It would be wonderful if Dad and I could go with you, but . . . well, maybe next time."

They got close to the school. Artie's teacher Mrs. Warfield was standing by the bus door. She had a clipboard in one hand and two freshly sharpened pencils in the other. She was checking in the students as they arrived. Most of the children were already waiting in line.

Everyone was wearing a nametag, even the teacher. Hers said "Mrs. Isabelle Warfield."

Artie stepped into line and she handed him his name tag; it read "Artie Willison." Mrs. Warfield checked and rechecked every child as they stood outside the bus. At eight o'clock on the dot, she checked them one more time and they all filed into their seats.

Chapter 4

Everyone was settled in, and the bus pulled out of the school parking lot.

Terry raised her hand and got Mrs. Warfield's attention. "Mrs. Warfield, Mrs. Warfield? May we sing a song on the way to the chocolate factory?"

"Well, yes that's a great idea, Terry. Do you have one in mind?"

"How about 'Peter Cottontail'?" Shannon shouted from the back of the bus.

"Oh, that's a good one." Shayna said. "It's all about jelly beans, eggs, chocolate bunnies, and Easter baskets. Easter's almost here, so that would be perfect."

"I bet we all know that one!" Jo spoke out.

Mrs. Warfield stood up and looked at the children. She paused for just a second, and then she said, "Well . . . before we get started singing this fun song, there might be a few of you who do not know the words. We all know 'Peter Cottontail' is an Easter song. Easter is a Christian holiday. Not all of us on the bus today are Christians, so someone sitting right next to you might not know the words to this song. If you don't know the words, you can go ahead and hum along if you'd like. First though, let's take just a minute before we start singing and see who might not know the words, and why.

"In our science class alone, we have many children from different religions of the world. Who can tell us what the three major world religions are?"

Kristin raised her hand. "I know, Mrs. Warfield."

"Okay, Kris, why don't you tell us what they are."

"Christianity, Islam, and Hinduism."

"That is absolutely correct, Kris. Good job."

Jay added, "There are lots more, but those are three of the largest religions."

"Thank you," Mrs. Warfield replied. Then she added, "Rachel and David celebrate Jewish holidays this time of year."

"Yes, Mrs. Warfield. It is our Passover celebration," Rachel said.

"Parviz and Parvin celebrate Islamic holidays," Mrs. Warfield said.

"That's right, Mrs. Warfield," Parviz said. "We pray and fast during the whole month of Ramadan. Then we celebrate Eid al-Fitr at the end of fasting. We have tasty treats. Gaz candy and Zoolbia, a lacy, fried pastry with honey, are two of my favorites. We also give thanks to God and help people in need by giving to the poor." Parviz smiled proudly.

"Oh, we do too!" David said. "We have gifts of sweet chocolate eggs and gold-wrapped chocolate coins after giving thanks at our traditional Passover dinner."

"We thank God for leading us out of slavery in Egypt," Rachel explained.

"Christians have chocolate eggs too! Most importantly, though, we celebrate the Lord Jesus," Sheri said.

Mrs. Warfield had a huge smile on her face. Looking a little like a child herself, she said, "We all love chocolate treats. And it doesn't matter what holidays we celebrate or if we're young or old, chocolate is something we all have in common. Today, we'll get to tour a factory that makes something for everyone." She looked around at her students. "Do you know that the chocolate factory we are going to tour today is a certified kosher factory? Who can tell us what that means?"

Aaron raised his hand. "I can try, Mrs. Warfield. Kosher means proper or acceptable. Kosher is food that is prepared in a certain way according to Jewish dietary laws."

"A little bit like vegetarians," Shaina blurted out from the middle of the bus.

"Yes," Ellie said. "It is strict, just like vegetarians. Vegetarians don't eat meat, and they keep to a very exact and strict diet too."

Casey raised her hand. "My sister Whitney is a vegan. She not only doesn't eat meat, but she also won't eat any animal products. She won't even wear anything made from any kind of animal. Now that is really strict!"

Summer waved her hand and finally got Mrs. Warfield's attention.

"Yes, Summer?" Mrs. Warfield asked.

Summer lowered her hand. "We only eat organic foods in our family! That means the food has been kept chemical free from the time the seeds are planted in the ground until the food is picked. That's pretty strict too."

Decker jumped in, "Hindus believe all life is sacred, so any meat is out of their diet, just like vegetarians and vegans. Hindus are non-violent to all life forms, even spiders and ants. Hinduism is also the oldest religion on earth."

"Yes, indeed," Mrs. Warfield agreed. "There are many different ways of life, children. These things make us all different, yet the same, not only in our faiths but even in simple everyday things like eating."

Kristy added, "American Indians and many other people enjoy the spirits of the earth, wind, and fire. It is not quite a religion as such, but a deep respect and love for all life."

Mrs. Warfield said, "Someday, I'm sure you'll all learn more about world religions and religious customs. For right now though, we will sing 'Peter Cottontail,' written by Steve Nelson and Jack Rollins. We'll sing a Passover and Eid al-Fitr song on the way home."

The children sang and clapped the rest of the way to the chocolate factory.

Here comes Peter Cottontail,
Hopping down the bunny trail,
Hippity, hoppity . . .

Chapter 5

The bus pulled into the chocolate factory parking lot.

"We're here; we're here! Yahoo!" everyone shouted.

"One at a time, children," Mrs. Warfield reminded the kids as they stood up to leave the bus.

Leon, their official chocolate factory tour guide for the day, greeted them. He had a giant smile on his face, and he held his arms wide open as if to hug each and every one of them as they stepped off the bus. "Good morning, children. I am so happy you're here!" And the way he said it, everyone knew he truly meant it.

"I hope you had a nice bus ride," Leon said. "We will have a great time today, and I am sure you and I will both learn a lot. Ask as many questions as you want. If I know the answer, I'll tell you. If I don't know the answer, I'll do my best to go find out what it is."

Everyone loved Leon right away!

Mabel was curious about Leon's name tag. "Is your name 'Mr. Leon'?"

Leon looked down at his name tag. "Oh no, kids. I have such a long, long Italian last name no one can pronounce it, so everyone just calls me Leon. That's what I'd like you all to do too."

Leon now became very serious, looking each child right in the eyes, he said, "Before we get started on the tour, I am going to tell you a very important story. I want you to think about what I'm going to share with you as we go along on the factory tour. Step by step, as we go through the factory, think about this story and imagine how it would be if it were to happen right here, this very day.

"While you are watching the chocolate bunnies being made, I want you to remember every single thing I tell you. Then, see if your heart can believe. Okay, kids. Are you ready to listen and listen very closely?" Leon asked.

"Yes, yes, Leon!" the kids called out. "We're ready! Tell us please." They could hardly wait to hear what Leon was going to tell them. Every single child, and even Mrs. Warfield, stood silently, all ears listening to Leon's voice and all eyes wide open as big as saucers, steadily gazing at his lips.

"Where do I begin?" Leon thought for a minute. "My new friends, let me start at the beginning. Well, the beginning as I know it, anyway."

Leon paused, considering the exact words he wanted to say. "There is a legend that has been told in all of the chocolate factories around the world for as long as I can remember. This legend has been passed down for many, many, many years. Until now, this story has only been shared with chocolate factory employees, but today I am going to share it with all of you.

"After today, you will all be able to share it with everyone you know. Then, everyone you know can share it with everyone they know. In the very near future, with the new chocolate character we are making right here in this chocolate factory, the whole world will know this wonderful story. Soon, it will be shared with everyone, and the whole wide world will know about this magical legend."

Leon took a breath. "Let's have everyone sit down here on these benches, and I will go on." He pointed to the benches. "Now, as I said before, let us all listen very carefully so we can think about this as we go on the tour. The chocolate factory's legend is this . . ."

Leon cleared his throat and began: "No one knows when, why, or how—in a chocolate factory somewhere in the world, in some country, in some town, city, or province—it could happen in any place that has a chocolate factory that makes chocolate rabbits. Once in a lifetime, one single molded chocolate rabbit is chosen out of all the rabbits being made, and that rabbit is given a very special gift. One and only one particular rabbit will be given this very special gift.

"The legend says this one chocolate rabbit is chosen to become the 'Real Chocolate Rabbit.' And this chocolate rabbit is given the gift . . . of life.

"Why this happens, no one knows. How many times it has happened, no one knows. How it happens, no one knows. The only thing that is known for sure is that it does, in fact, happen. And when it does, it is a gift not only to the chocolate rabbit that becomes real, but a gift to everyone in the world. This special little rabbit has powers that appear when we believe. Powers that will help him stay alive. Our belief in him gives him strength, and that strength is what helps him in times of great danger. It also keeps him going when life seems too hard."

Chapter 6

"Wow, Leon! What does that mean exactly?" Teri asked. "How could that happen?"

"Yeah, Leon," Keane questioned. "How could a chocolate rabbit become real? Gee, you mean real chocolate, not imitation chocolate? A kind of catchy word thing, or something like that, right?"

"Nope," Leon said. "Not at all, Keane. It is not a word thing or a trick saying. The legend says that one chocolate rabbit, out of all of the millions, actually billions, that are made each year in chocolate factories all around the world, actually becomes a real living furry rabbit. One of the chocolate bunnies being made right here today, right before your eyes, *could* be the ONE. One of these chocolate rabbits could be the Real Chocolate Rabbit."

"Golly," Keane said thoughtfully.

"Really, Leon? Really?" Soleil asked. "Leon, do you really believe that?"

"You know, Soleil, I honestly do!" Leon replied. "I truly believe it. I feel it in my heart. Soleil, I believe you will believe it too!

"There is something else we all have to do." Leon went on, "The legend says that every time we see a rabbit, any bunny rabbit, we must say, '*I believe.*' But we cannot just say it though; we must also truly believe it in our hearts. Every time we see a bunny and say, 'I believe,' all the Real Chocolate Rabbits in the world somehow feel it, and they gain strength wherever in the world they are. And the stronger each Real Chocolate Rabbit gets, the more they are helped in times of danger. That strength gives them special powers to survive.

"Rabbits have very unique little hearts; they are loving, kind, and very gentle. There is almost no room in a bunny's heart for strength because it is all filled up with love and goodness. A rabbit's little heart is so giving and tender that it gets scared and overwhelmed easily. When a bunny gets scared, its little heart beats so hard and so fast that it usually gives out on it in times of danger. You see, to the pure of heart, all things are good, so bad things in life are terrifying for these little guys. The very best thing we can do to help these rabbits is to believe enough to say 'I believe' every time we see one.

"When we see a bunny rabbit and say, 'I believe,' strength spills into their hearts and makes them stronger. The power we give them with our belief allows them to live longer, and it keeps them safe and out of harm's way. Sometimes, like magic, it will keep these exceptional little creatures protected in times of peril.

"That is how all the Real Chocolate Rabbits everywhere survive. It is the *only* way they survive. This is what we humans can do for these wonderful little rabbit critters—it is our gift to them. And, in turn, they are a special gift to us. When people believe in all the goodness these little rabbits have and say so out loud, all the Real Chocolate Rabbits can live on and on. So, tell everyone you know to say 'I believe' every time they see a bunny. Spread the word, okay?"

"What about a spotted bunny, Leon?" Curran asked. "Does it work with them?"

"Yes, of course," Leon answered.

Deb asked, "What about a reddish bunny?"

Leon smiled and replied, "Yes. Light brown, tan, chocolate-brown, light-colored, gray, white, even multicolored. Any color of rabbit at all."

"What about a jackrabbit, Leon?" Klarissa asked. "Does it work then?"

"Yes, it does," Leon replied.

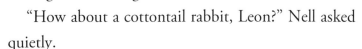

"What about a flop-eared or dwarf bunny, Leon?" Elaine asked waving her hand high in the air.

"How about a cottontail rabbit, Leon?" Nell asked quietly.

"Yes, yes, and yes to all colors and all kinds of bunny rabbits and hares," Leon said. "As long as you believe.

"In the rabbit world, my friends, all rabbits and hares are equal, no matter what their color, size, or shape. Someday, wouldn't it be nice if that were true for everyone?"

Leon continued. "One day—or maybe it has already happened, we really do not know—a Real Chocolate Rabbit will be strong enough and live

long enough to meet up with another Real Chocolate Rabbit, and they will be friends."

"You mean like girlfriend and boyfriend, Leon?" Aspen asked. Before he could answer, she blurted out, "Wow, maybe they could even have a whole big Real Chocolate Rabbit family. What do you think, Leon?"

"Well, I never even thought of anything like that," he said. "I guess anything can happen when we believe!"

Every one of the children looked at Leon, and they knew he meant every word he was saying. Leon believed, and now, so did they!

"Leon?" This time it was Chloe who raised her hand. "Did you say it is only bunnies that are made in this factory that can become real?"

"Oh, no, no. Real Chocolate Rabbits can be made in any chocolate factory that makes chocolate rabbits anywhere in the world. There might be a factory clear across the ocean making one right this second. But now, let's get this tour started. What do you say, my friends?"

"Yes, yes, Leon!" all the children shouted at the same time. "Let's go!"

Chapter 7

The children walked to the factory entrance, and Leon explained a little bit about tempering chocolate. "When you all get back from spring break," he explained, "Mrs. Warfield has some paperwork on the melting, cooling, and agitation it takes to temper chocolate. The exact science of it is way too much to go into today. That's for your next science lesson in school.

"Today, the thing you can keep in mind is that, in order to get our chocolate not to melt in our hands when we hold it, and for all our products to be crisp and shiny, the chocolate we use must be tempered chocolate. We use the tempering process for everything we make here. Your science class is a wonderful place to learn all the specifics when you get back to school."

The tour began, and each of the children looked with wide-eyed wonder and paid close attention to every detail of how the bunnies were being made. Artie paid extra close attention so he could tell Jaymee exactly how everything was done, just as she had asked him to do. They all watched as the huge pots of liquid tempered chocolate poured the exact amount into each plastic mold. Then they watched as the molds were snapped together and spun so fast that all the chocolate landed smoothly and evenly on the inside of the mold, leaving a beautiful, hollow chocolate bunny. Hollow, that is, except for the ears, because the ears were thinner than the rabbits' bodies, so the chocolate poured into the ear parts of the molds and stayed thick and solid with the sweet chocolate. Yum.

Everyone wondered as they watched, *Is that the one? Could this one be the one? What about that one? Could it become the Real Chocolate Rabbit?* Almost at the end of the tour, they watched as the workers glued the little eyes onto the faces of the blank rabbits. A little dab of warm melted chocolate, one for each candy eye, and like magic, the bunnies had faces. Another dab of soft chocolate to hold the colored bow underneath the rabbit's chin, then one more dollop to fasten the orange candy carrot in their paws.

Voilà! The bunnies were finished.

Every one of the children studied each rabbit for any hint that it might be the *one*. They looked for anything different . . . anything, even a tiny speck that might indicate it would someday be the Real Chocolate Rabbit.

Now, at the very end of the tour, everyone stared as the finished rabbits were carefully slipped into boxes. For the last time, everyone looked at every detail to see if they could tell if there was any difference, any mark that made one chocolate bunny look any different from the others. They watched, and they thought, and they watched some more.

Could that one be the one? Or that one?

When the tour was over, Leon walked them from the factory to just outside of the main lobby. Everyone was excited and chattering all at once to each other about how much they had learned and how fun it had been. Each one of them thought that they, in fact, had seen the one rabbit that was going to be the Real Chocolate Rabbit. The children all compared notes, but none of them could agree on the same bunny. Besides, there were so-o-o-o-o-o many!

As they headed for the lobby. Leon explained he had a surprise for them and that they should all go carefully, two by two, to the far side of the room. He told them to stand over by the large table against the wall—the table with the purple cloth covering it.

Artie started to go into the lobby, but he noticed Albert sitting on the ground, crying. Leon noticed Albert too, so they both walked over to see what was wrong. The other children went ahead into the lobby with Mrs. Warfield.

Albert was sobbing. Artie knelt on one knee and asked, "Albert, what's wrong?"

When Albert was finally able to spit out the words, he said, "My wallet! My wallet is gone!" Then he sobbed some more.

"Oh, Albert," Artie tried to assure him and said, "It must be here somewhere. I'll go back and look for it, okay? Please don't cry anymore, Albert. I'll find it for you."

"Artie, that is very thoughtful of you," Leon said.

Albert looked up at Artie and wiped his eyes and then his nose. "Gee, thanks," he said. "That's swell of you, Artie."

Artie turned around and started retracing the path they had just come from, all the way back to the factory door.

Chapter 8

 Leon took Albert by the hand, and the two of them walked inside to join the others in the lobby. Everyone was waiting at the table with Mrs. Warfield.

"All right, my friends. Here we go. Remember: the whole reason for this class tour is because we are promoting a new chocolate character this year. And you get the *very* first look at our new chocolate creation. He is modeled after the rabbit I told you about in the legend . . ."

Leon grabbed the edge of the purple cloth that covered the table, and in one swoop, he whisked the cloth away. "Ta-da!" The whole table was uncovered. "My friends, meet . . . the Real Chocolate Rabbit!"

Every inch of the table was covered with beautifully boxed, ten-ounce chocolate rabbits. The headline at the top of each cardboard box read "The Real Chocolate Rabbit." In each box was the best-looking chocolate rabbit any of the kids had ever seen. It was enormous, and attached to the rabbit's side was a large, golden-colored chocolate star. The star was stamped in the middle with the words "I believe."

Oh, they all knew that this chocolate bunny was so grand that none of them would be able to afford to buy one, even when they went on sale in the stores. This was a very special chocolate rabbit that only a very few people would ever be able to have, they thought. They gazed longingly at the large bunnies staring back at them.

"Come on, children," Leon said. "Step a little closer to the table. I want you to get a good look."

All the children, almost spellbound, stepped a little closer, their eyes opened wide and their mouths gaping a bit with amazement.

"Wow, they are wonderful, Leon!" Ruth said.

"Well, my friends," Leon exclaimed "are you ready for the best part?"

The children hardly heard Leon because they were so dazzled by the big beautiful rabbits.

Leon tried again. "Well, kids, are you ready for the best part?"

"Oh, yes. Okay," the children finally replied, still in a daze. "Alright, what is the best part, Leon?"

"Well, my friends, there is one bunny for each of you to take home today."

Everyone started talking at once.

"Oh, my gosh, Leon!" "No way." "Holy cow." "Really, Leon? Really?" "Are you kidding?" "Oh, my golly!" "Yippee!" "Wow, each one of us gets one of these humongous chocolate bunnies?"

Everyone jumped up and down. They could hardly believe it.

"Yes," Leon said. "Believe it!"

The kids squealed with delight. Nothing could be better than this.

"Okay, now," Leon said. "Come on. Carefully, one at a time, reach over and get your rabbit."

Just as the last child grabbed his rabbit, Artie called from the door. "Albert, Albert! I found it! I've got your wallet!"

As each of the children hugged their rabbits, they turned to see Artie, walking across the lobby toward them.

"Hey, what's going on? What have you got?" he asked.

"Artie, we all get one. We all get to take home one of these huge, beautiful chocolate rabbits. Look at the star, Artie. It says, 'I believe.' And look at the name, Artie. 'The Real Chocolate Rabbit,' just like the one Leon told us about in the legend."

Oh goodness, Artie thought, *wishes do come true after all!* Artie's heart was pounding. He was so thrilled. He thought, *Wow, we can finally give something to Grandpa and Nana this year!* He could never have even wished for such a grand gift for them.

As he got closer to everyone, he handed Albert his wallet. Then he turned to make his way to the table. When he walked past the other children, he looked at the table and…well, it was empty.

Artie wasn't worried though, because this was his lucky day. First, he'd found Albert's wallet, and now he was going to be able to take a marvelous chocolate bunny to his grandparents all the way in Minden, Nevada.

Chapter 9

"Leon," James said. "What about Artie? The table is empty. Where is Artie's chocolate rabbit?"

Leon's face turned pale. He quickly counted the rabbits that the children were holding, then looked back at the empty table. "Oh no, this can't be! This just isn't right. We had a final count. What happened?"

He looked again at the empty table. "We're one rabbit short! There are no more. The factory made these especially for your class! This is terrible. There is nothing I can do."

Leon looked sadly at Artie and said, "You won't even be able to buy one of these rabbits this year. They will not be going into production until next year, and that is only if all the big bosses approve them. Oh, Artie, I am so very sorry."

Artie looked at Leon. He held his breath because he knew he was ready to cry, but he sure didn't want to.

He blinked a couple of times and bit the inside of his lower lip, just the slightest.

"Maybe someone will give you their rabbit, Artie," Leon proposed. "After all, you missed out because you were doing something nice by walking back to find Albert's wallet. It doesn't seem fair you should lose out for being kind."

Each and every one of the kids, and especially Albert, felt bad for Artie, but they all looked at their rabbits and then at each other, with fear in their eyes.

Oh my gosh, they were all thinking. *Am I going to have to give up my rabbit? Will Leon take mine and give it to Artie?*

The fear kept welling up inside, as each one imagined it might be them who would lose their rabbit. As sad as they were for Artie, they all pulled their rabbit boxes a little closer and clutched them a little tighter.

Artie spoke up. "No, Leon, please. That wouldn't be right. Let everyone keep their rabbits."

"But, Artie—"

"No," Artie said again. "I could never do that. It wouldn't be fair." Artie said it so firmly he almost believed it himself—but not quite. Inside, he was all broken up.

Artie's mind raced as he thought about how happy he had been just thinking about giving this perfect rabbit to Nana Jean and Grandpa Art. He tried to shake it from his head so no one would see how truly brokenhearted he was, but he wasn't sure he could.

Everyone looked away from Artie and over to Leon to see what he was going to say. It was so quiet you could hear almost everyone breathing. Mrs. Warfield though, held her breath and waited to see what would happen.

Artie looked at Leon. He knew he had done the right thing, but oh, how he would have loved to have one of those grand, big bunnies for his grandparents.

"Well, Artie, that's a mighty fine thing you are doing!" Leon said. "And it's your decision, so we'll respect it. We will leave it at that then, kids. Other than to say, I'm sorry, Artie. I just do not know what could have happened."

One by one, the kids filed by Artie and hugged him and thanked him.

Artie hugged them all back, as he fought back his tears.

"Leon?" Artie asked.

"Yes? What is it, kiddo?"

"My sister Jaymee and I put together a little over four dollars, and I was wondering if there is something like an egg or a pack of chocolate gold coins I could buy and take to our grandparents in Minden?"

"I'm so sorry, Artie. I wish there were, but the factory only makes orders for stores. There is nothing for sale here. Not a single thing."

"Oh well, Leon. It was just a thought."

Leon stood very still for a moment.

Everyone could see he was thinking. No one said a word; they just stared at him.

Then Leon said, "Wait a minute, my friends I need to check on something." He looked at Mrs. Warfield. "Will you stay right here with the children until I get back?"

"Yes, of course." Mrs. Warfield looked at Leon, then at the kids, and then back at Leon.

They all wondered where Leon was going and what kind of an idea he had, so all eyes followed him as he left the room. They saw that Leon was talking to someone on his cell phone as he hurried back toward the factory.

Chapter 10

Leon, still talking on his phone, made his way back to the factory. He hurried back to an area near the trash dock. Talking into his phone he said, "Yes, I'm here . . . Yes, I can see the crusher. If it's okay with you, I can grab one before it's too late. There are only a few left on the conveyor belt. Oh great! Thanks! That's fantastic! And just in time, I hope. Thank you. Thank you very much. This is going to mean so much to that young man. Thank you again."

Leon scanned the conveyor belt as he stood at the trash dock. All the boxes on the conveyor belt were headed straight for the crusher. His eyes darted from one box to another. Each rabbit in every box had cracked or broken ears. That was exactly why the box design had been abandoned, and exactly why a new, better box had been fabricated.

Kaboom. Kaboom.

The crusher machine made its loud *kaboom* as it smashed the boxes, one by one, at the end of the belt.

Kaboom.

Leon's ears hurt, but he kept looking.

There's got to be one, he thought. *I just need one. There! There's one!*

Kaboom. Kaboom.

Leon dashed over to the conveyor belt and just before the machine could thunder down and smash the box and the rabbit in it, Leon reached out and grabbed it.

Kaboom. Just in time.

Woo, he thought, *that was a close call, but I got it.*

Leon carefully—very carefully—examined the chocolate rabbit inside the clear cellophane window. He wanted to be sure it was not cracked or broken like all the others had been.

Well, he thought, *this one looks perfect*. He was so happy, he grinned from ear to ear.

Leon hurried back through the door, holding the large chocolate bunny. The rabbit looked exactly like the ones all the children were holding, only there was a clear cellophane puffy window on the top of his box, it was closed at the top with a plastic-coated twist tie.

The bottom portion was the only thing that was cardboard. It was an extremely odd-looking box. He carried it very carefully at the bottom, holding only the cardboard portion so he wouldn't break the rabbit or the rabbit's big ears.

Leon was very excited and said, "I just talked to the big bosses, Artie. I told them we were one rabbit short in our giveaway and that while you were doing a deed of kindness, you missed out on getting one. I asked them if there was anything we could do to make up it up to you. They talked it over and said I could look at all the broken rabbits that were on the way to the crusher and see if there were any that were not ruined. If I could find one in perfect condition, I could give it to you."

Leon held up the box. "As you can see, it is the same chocolate rabbit character as everyone else has. Only the box is different. This one is from the first design, but because they used so much clear cellophane on the top, the rabbits were breaking too easily, so they stopped production and made a new box.

"Company policy is to destroy any defective or damaged products, so all the broken rabbits in the old packaging were on their way to the crusher, and then to the garbage. I could hardly believe my eyes when I saw this one. There he was: one perfect rabbit. I snagged it right off the conveyor belt, right before the crusher had a chance to smash it. *Kaboom* is the noise the crusher makes."

Leon held out the box. "Here, Artie, this one is for you." He handed Artie the giant chocolate rabbit in the odd-looking package.

"Oh, Leon, thank you. Thank you so much. This is the best! You are the best! Thank the big bosses too, would ya please, Leon?"

The instant Artie laid his eyes on that chocolate rabbit, he knew it was special; he knew it was just for him. Even before Leon said a word, he knew it in his heart. This chocolate rabbit was meant to be his.

Leon kept talking, but Artie did not hear a word he was saying. Artie was so happy, he was in a daze as he gazed at his rabbit and hugged it gently.

Everyone was so excited for Artie. They all cheered, "hip, hip, hooray" and jumped up and down for joy.

For just a fleeting nanosecond, Artie thought how nice it would be if he could keep the chocolate rabbit for himself and give it to his mom, dad, and Jaymee, but he knew he couldn't. This rabbit was for Nana

Jean and Grandpa Art. His heart ached a little as he looked into his rabbit's face, knowing he would only have it for a short time. Then Artie thought, *I'm so happy right now. I will just be happy having the rabbit and being able to take it all the way to Minden. I'll get to enjoy him during the plane ride and in the car. Oh, won't Jaymee be happy too when she sees this magnificent chocolate rabbit!*

All the students shook Leon's hand as they got back onto the bus.

Boy, they all loved Leon and the story about the "Real Chocolate Rabbit." Leon stood and waved at the children as they peered out the bus windows, waving back until Leon was but a speck standing on the curb.

Chapter 11

Artie hung onto the big chocolate bunny all the way to the airport. Artie's mom had placed the rabbit in a large blue bag so Artie could carry it onto the airplane without a problem, and she tied a red, metallic ribbon to the top. It looked great.

"Thanks, Mom," Artie said. He and Jaymee reached out to both their mom and dad and gave them a huge hug goodbye.

This was the first time Jaymee and Artie had ever traveled anywhere without their parents, so they hugged them one more time before they started boarding the plane. Artie and Jaymee were both excited but a little frightened at the same time about the plane ride, and also about leaving their mom and dad for the first time. But they had each other and the best chocolate rabbit in the world, so they could hardly wait for the plane to fly them to Nevada to see their grandparents. They looked back one more time at their mom and dad.

"Love you!" They said, then they turned and got on the plane.

Chapter 12

"Nana! Nana! Grandpa!" Artie and Jaymee raced over to their grandparents. "Nana Jean! Grandpa Art! We have missed you so-o-o-o-o-o much since you moved. We are so glad to be here finally!"

"Oh, kids," Nana Jean said, beaming, "you'll never know how much it means for us to see you both again. We have missed you and your mom and dad every day since we moved."

They all hugged each other for a long time.

"Come on, now," said Nana Jean, "We want to hear all about your trip when we get into the car. It's about a forty-five-minute ride from here in Reno to Minden. We can wait here while Grandpa gets the Jeep."

"Grandpa, look!" Artie shouted. "Is that a hawk over there?" He pointed at a huge, dark brownish bird sitting on a post.

"Yes, indeed, Artie. It's a hawk alright, and a big one at that."

"Grandpa, what kind of hawk is it?" Artie asked.

"Really can't say for sure, kiddo. They all pretty much look the same to me—brown with some reddish color in them, like that one. If I had to guess, I would say it is a red-tailed hawk. Look at its tail color if he flies. We have a lot of hawks in the valley; could be some other kind of hawk. Your grandma has a nice bird book, so we can look through it when we get home. That hawk is unusual though; bigger than most and much darker than I have ever seen before. Gives him an almost menacing look, don't you think? Wouldn't want to mess with that one."

Grandpa laughed at the thought, and then he said, "Keep your eyes open on the way home for more hawks, Artie. You might see some."

Grandpa Art walked into the parking garage. A few minutes later, he pulled up in a metallic red Jeep, almost the exact same color as the ribbon that was tied around the rabbit's bag. Red was Grandpa Art's favorite color. Artie's mom must have picked out that color ribbon on purpose just for him.

Clutching the rabbit bag, Artie stood behind

Jaymee, trying to use her to stay out of the wind. But the wind was whisking through the parking area; there was no way of getting away from it, no matter how he tried. The top of the big bag began to rustle and whip around.

Whoosh.

A large gust of wind came up, and the bright red metallic ribbon came untied. It swirled and flew way up into the air. The wind was so strong, neither Artie nor Jaymee could grab the ribbon before it whirled up, up, up, and away. Jaymee and Artie watched as it just kept flying higher and higher, until it was just . . . gone.

Chapter 13

Something caught the hawk's eye as he sat looking over the Reno airport. It was a brightly colored red ribbon whirling in the wind. *Where did that come from?* he wondered.

He looked down at all the cars. There were cars, but no people. He circled. Then he saw it—a red Jeep with humans standing by it. The two little humans were looking up into the sky, while the two bigger ones were loading things inside the Jeep. It was the only car around that had people. The little boy standing there was clutching something inside a blue bag. The wind kept lapping at the bag he held. The top of the bag was waving in the wind.

I bet that red ribbon came from that blue bag. Hmm, but wait, what's that? It wasn't the bag that was intriguing to the hawk; it was something inside the bag. As the wind kept pulling the bag down further and further, the hawk could see more and more of what was inside. Something of much more importance was inside—more important than that bright red ribbon flying in the air or the blue flapping bag. *Let me see what that is*, he thought.

The hawk dove down to get a closer look. Closer and closer he flew. Then he saw it! The wind blew the blue bag open just enough for him to peek inside, just enough for him to see a huge pair of rabbit ears. The rabbit ears were in a box with a clear cellophane top, so he saw only the very tip of the ears clearly, and only for a second before the wind whipped the bag back up.

Oh my golly, the hawk thought. *A beautiful bunny must be attached to those ears! Oh, how wonderful it would be to have a big fat rabbit for dinner.* He knew right then and there he had to have that rabbit.

But wait, what was that little boy doing? He was putting the whole bag with the box and the bunny into the back of that Jeep. *Oh no, no, no, no,* thought the hawk. *He can't do that. I want that bunny. I need that bunny. I have to have that huge, beautiful, delectable bunny.*

The hawk swooped down as low as he could, but there was no way he could get his claws on the bag. The big man person slammed the hatch door shut and off the red Jeep went down the road. *Oh my,* the hawk thought, *I've got no choice. I have to follow them. I'll trail them to the ends of the earth. I have to have that rabbit.*

The hawk could see just a tiny glimpse of the top of the bunny's ears through the back window. *There is something different about that rabbit,* he thought. *Why is that rabbit in a box and not out hopping around where I can get to it?*

The hawk did not know. He just knew he needed to follow, watch, and wait. He would have his moment; he would not take his eyes off this prize until he did.

The hawk circled the Jeep from high in the sky. When the Jeep went fast, he went fast. When the Jeep turned, he turned. When the Jeep stopped, he stopped. When the Jeep started again, so did he. The hawk followed and followed and followed.

Chapter 14

Artie and Jaymee talked nonstop with their grandparents all the way to Minden. When they finally got to Minden and looked up at Jobs Peak and the incredible Sierra Nevada mountain range, they saw for themselves exactly what Nana Jean and Grandpa Art had been telling them for the past year: Minden indeed was just a "footstep from the Sierras." How beautiful the mountains looked. They had never seen anything like them. The fields were so green. Neither of them had ever seen alfalfa fields before—or cows, much less longhorn steer. What fantastic sights. This was Nevada!

They got to the house, and Artie and Jaymee were so excited they grabbed their things to take inside, and then they saw… IT…the barn.

"Holy cow, a real barn!" Artie said.

"You never told us you had a barn, Nana! Oh my goodness, a barn!"

"Can we go and look inside?" they both asked together. "Oh please, Nana, Grandpa, can we?"

"Yes, of course," Nana answered. "You can go right now. Come on back to the house when you're done looking, and we'll get something to eat."

Dropping everything they had in their arms behind the Jeep, Artie and Jaymee ran as fast as they could toward the barn. They left the blue bag with the chocolate rabbit sitting next to their two small suitcases and a blanket from the Jeep.

A shadow on the ground caught Artie's eye. He looked up at the sky and saw a hawk circling. *Wow*, he thought, *that hawk looks just like the one we saw at the*

airport. He laughed at himself and shook his head from side to side. *Nah, that couldn't be; they don't fly that far.* Grandpa said there were lots of hawks in the valley.

Artie looked away from the huge raptor and chased after Jaymee back toward the barn.

Chapter 15

The hawk was nearly exhausted as he followed the red Jeep up a long dirt road then finally, the Jeep stopped.

Oh, thank goodness! he thought. *Look! A tree I can sit in. I can finally rest.* He barely made it to the nearest branch of the enormous sycamore across the street from the parked red Jeep. His wings throbbed so badly, he feared they would drop off and he'd be wingless for life.

He rested in the cool shade of the tree. He watched all the commotion around the Jeep as the humans got out and unloaded the trunk. He saw the two little ones race toward a big barn in the backyard. Even though he was exhausted, he decided to fly over and take a look, and that's when he caught sight of it. The hawk's heart stopped beating for a second as he spotted the ears. He could barely see them inside the blue bag.

Yes, yes, indeed. There are the ears. He looked harder

for a fat bunny, but all he could see were the tips of the ears because the bag covered the rest.

Yes, what a fine tasty rabbit. All for me.

Everyone had gone, and there it was, sitting all alone next to the suitcases and a rumpled-up blanket. He knew this was his chance—maybe the only chance he would ever have to get that rabbit. He didn't have much time. In a split second, throbbing wings and all, he darted toward the Jeep.

He could taste that rabbit already. He was so excited as he got closer and closer, he could hardly keep his thoughts straight. His heart was pounding and his huge wings were still hurting, but with the precision of a brain surgeon, he twisted his body, took aim, and his strong talons reached down and…

WHAM!

His razor-sharp claws made a direct hit and locked onto the top of the cellophane. He grabbed hold and jerked with all his force, and at long last, it was done. He had his trophy.

He turned around and started climbing higher and higher into the sky. He climbed almost to the sun with his prized possession. The hawk looked back at the empty blue bag lying on the ground and then swung east towards the Pine Nut Mountains. In a few minutes, he would find the wide-open range to have this mouthwatering, delightful dinner.

Chapter 16

As tired as the hawk was, he flew the best he could with the box weighing him down. The box got heavier and heavier. The hawk was now painfully tired, but he couldn't stop. He wanted an area where there were no houses, no cars, and no people so he would not be disturbed while enjoying this wonderful, tasty meal. A wide-open space with no trees or bushes.

All of a sudden, it was too much for him. His talons weakened their grip. He struggled to hold on, but as hard as he tried, he could not. He tried and tried to make it over the trees and bushes, but no—the box with the rabbit was oh so heavy now. Despite his best effort, the box slipped out of his grasp and started plummeting to the ground.

The hawk knew, from the height he was flying, that the box, the rabbit—everything—would be shattered into smithereens once it hit the earth. He could not bear to look. He had come so far for this tasty meal.

But look he did, and he could not believe what he saw. As the box fell, air rushed into it from the bottom, and the cellophane at the top of the box filled up with air like a hot air balloon. The box, and the rabbit in it, gently floated down toward the ground. Slowly it drifted and drifted, finally sinking into a thick sagebrush bush.

The hawk dove down to take a better look so he could remember exactly what bush the box had landed in. He would come back to get it when he wasn't quite so tired. But *poof!* The box with the rabbit had disappeared.

The hawk circled and swooped really low. He was so dreadfully tired, but he needed to see where that box had landed. The hawk then sat in a tall pine tree and looked some more.

He looked and looked, but it was as if the box had been swallowed up. He could not see a trace, not even a hint of where it had gone.

Strange, he thought. *How could the whole thing just disappear? Where is that rabbit? Where is that box? What a blow to come this far and never have even gotten a taste of that big bunny's ear. I will come back tomorrow and figure out exactly what happened, and I will find that box and the succulent bunny rabbit!*

He was far too tired and hungry to spend one more second looking for the rabbit now. The hawk flew back toward the valley the same way he'd come. As he passed over the house where he had grabbed the rabbit, he saw the little boy running around, looking here and there.

Silly little boy, he thought. *You will never ever find that bunny or the box that it's in. Ha, ha. But I will tomorrow!*

He landed in the huge sycamore tree to watch and rest. He chuckled some more as the little boy started to cry and call for his sister.

Chapter 17

Artie ran from the back of the Jeep and into the house, calling for Jaymee. "Jaymee, Jaymee!"

She wasn't there.

"Nana, where is Jaymee?" Artie began to cry.

"What is it, Artie?" Nana Jean asked. "What's wrong, honey?"

"Nana, Oh, Nana. We brought the best present for you and Grandpa: a huge chocolate rabbit just for you and Grandpa Art. Oh, it was the very, very best. The best chocolate rabbit in the whole world, Nana, and it's gone. I can't find it anywhere." Tears rolled down Artie's cheeks, and he could not stop them.

"Artie, what do you mean it's gone? How? How could it be gone? Where was it, honey?" Nana Jean walked over to Artie and wrapped her arms tightly around him.

Artie could barely get the words out, his lips were

trembling so much. "It was behind the Jeep, Nana, and now it's not there. It's gone. We brought a wonderful gift for you and Grandpa, and it's gone. Nana, where could it be?"

Nana reached over to the tissue box and pulled out a handful of tissues. She put them up to Artie's face. Right away, the tissues got soggy from soaking up the stream of tears flowing from Artie's now-swollen brown eyes.

"I got it for you at the chocolate factory." Artie sniffled. "Just for you and Grandpa Art. It was a special bunny, Nana, very special. Oh, Nana, we have to find that rabbit!" Artie began sobbing again.

"Oh, Artie," Nana said. "I'm sure we'll be able to find it. It could not have just up and flown away."

"Nana, where could it have gone? We have to find it. Jaymee, Jaymee!" Artie cried out. "Where are you, Jaymee? Come help us."

"Art!" Nana called out this time. "Jaymee, come on in here for a minute, will you? Something has happened, and we need your help."

All four of them went outside and looked behind the red Jeep. There was nothing except the two suitcases and the empty blue bag the rabbit had been in and the blanket from the Jeep. Artie picked up the bag and said, "See, Nana, this is it; the bag Mom gave us. It had the chocolate rabbit in it. See, see, it was right here."

They looked and looked all around the Jeep. Grandpa Art even got into the Jeep and moved it forward a few feet, just in case they were missing something underneath. They walked farther and farther away from the Jeep, but still nothing. They couldn't find anything, not even a trace of the box or the chocolate bunny.

Grandpa Art took Artie's hand and went one way. Nana Jean took Jaymee's hand and went the other way. They walked and walked until they finally came full circle and ended up in the exact spot they had started. They still saw nothing.

They never found the box, the rabbit, or any sign of where it could have gone. The only thing there was the empty blue bag lying on the ground. The rabbit and box had just vanished. It was indeed a mystery.

"It's getting dark Artie. We need to go in. I'm sorry, but we have to quit for the night. I don't know where else to look. Honey, we will take look in the morning, before we go up to Lake Tahoe, okay? It's too dark out here now. Anyway, we will all be fresher in the morning to take another look."

Nana took Artie's hand, grandpa took Jaymee's and they all went into the house for the night.

Chapter 18

The box with the rabbit landed ever so softly into the waiting arms of a large, full sagebrush bush. The bush had velvety new growth, so the landing was gentle. As quickly as possible, the bush's limbs covered the box and the rabbit in it, hiding them under its silvery greenish-gray branches. The huge hawk that circled above never saw a thing.

As night fell and the wind blew, the bush wrapped its branches tighter and cradled the box to keep it and the little bunny inside safe from harm. As the night got colder, the bush wrapped more branches around the box to keep the little bunny warm. The bush embraced its special little package throughout the whole night.

The bright, shining moon and all the millions of stars in the sky seemed to be watching over the little rabbit too. They all were keeping their eyes on the precious little treasure in the funny-looking box. In the morning light, the box and bunny were still tucked safe and sound in the arms of the bush.

Neither the wind nor the cold evening temperatures had bothered the little chocolate rabbit in the least thanks to the protective arms of the native plant.

Chapter 19

About a mile away from where the box was cradled in the bush, a black bear cub was sound asleep under a pinion pine tree. When the sun poked its head over the top of the mountains and started to warm the big cub's body, the cub's nose began to twitch. Though he was still, for the most part, asleep, a sweet smell in his nostrils began to awaken him. At first, he thought he was still dreaming—dreaming of some magnificently sweet food—but his big bear nose kept twitching.

His nose continued to twitch, then to smell, then twitch, then smell, and the aroma in his dream got sweeter and sweeter and stronger and stronger, until it finally woke him up totally. Once he was fully awake and realized he was not dreaming any longer, he noticed that his nose was still twitching. What he was smelling was not a dream at all, but something real from down the hill! He sat straight up and sniffed some more, and then he let his big bear nose lead the way toward this wonderful scent.

He walked and walked, all the time letting his sniffing nose do the searching. It was leading him closer and closer to the heavenly sweet smell, which kept getting stronger and stronger. The scent was finally so strong he started looking with his eyes, instead of just his nose. He knew he was close. The smell was so powerful he could almost taste it.

Where was it coming from? It seemed to be coming from that bush. *That is crazy*, he thought. He had been here a thousand times and never had such a smell come from one of these bushes. He closed his eyes, turned around two times, and once again let his nose do the work for him. His nose led him directly back to the same bush.

Hmm, I'll take a closer look now. He looked and looked but saw nothing.

The sagebrush did its best to keep the box and the bunny hidden, but when the bear's large paws with those big dagger-sharp claws started spreading its branches, there was nothing the bush could do. The bear's paws were huge, and his claws cut through some of the bush's tender shoots. Then the box was exposed.

"Aha, there," said the bear out loud. "There you are, you wonderful smell. Let's have a look at you." He pulled the box from the entwined branches, leaving a hole where the box had been.

Oh my gosh! he thought. *This is it! This is what bears only imagine finding in their entire lifetimes. This is CHOCOLATE. Oh, I know no one will ever believe I have found chocolate; it is what bears only dream of finding. I'll take it with me and show it to everyone. I will be the king of bears when they see what I have found. Oh boy, oh boy!*

He paused. *Wait a minute. If I take it to the other bears, they will want to see it. Then they will want to touch it. Then they will want to taste it, and then they will eat it all before I even get a chance to take a bite. I won't do that. I don't care if no one believes me. This heavenly smelling chocolate is mine. I will eat it myself and then I will take the box to them as proof that I really found chocolate. I will be king bear cub.*

The bear cub raised the box to his lips. He thought about tearing the cellophane away, but he could hardly wait another second. He opened his mouth as wide open as he could. He closed his eyes really, really tight and was just getting ready to chomp off the chocolate rabbit's ears, when—

Chapter 20

At the same time, somewhere in the world at a chocolate factory, the workers were waiting for the factory gates to open, when they saw a rabbit run along the fence. They all shouted with joy from deep inside their hearts, "I believe, I believe!" At the exact second they called out, "I believe," the bear cub felt the box he was holding move.

What? he thought. *What is this? A box can't move.*

The cub was too scared to open his eyes, so he once again opened his mouth to take a bite.

Then, eeks!!

Not only did he feel the box move, but it wiggled; he actually felt something inside the box jump. It scared him so much that he tossed the box to the ground and scrambled behind a tree. The bear cub waited for a minute, but then very slowly opened his right eye, just a little, to take a peek. He saw the box lying on its side in a small clearing. It lay there, as still as can be.

Oh, it must have been the wind that fooled me, the bear thought. *That is the only thing that could have made the box move. I'll go over and get it now.*

How silly I am. I'm glad no one was here to see me acting like a fool, a scaredy bear." He laughed at himself.

The cub came out from behind the tree and walked toward the box. When he was about one foot away from the box, he could see inside the cellophane window. What he saw made his heart almost climb out of his chest. He stared at the box in disbelief.

Inside the box—where the sweet, yummy chocolate bunny had been—there was now a furry, fuzzy, long-eared *real* rabbit!

The bear cub looked again, still not believing his eyes. There it was—a real, breathing, nose-twitching rabbit, trying to hide in the bottom of the box.

The bear shrieked so loud the birds in the trees scattered like dust in the wind. The bear cub started to run. He could not run fast enough. He never once looked back. He never once told anyone in the world what had happened.

That was too crazy, he thought. *No one will ever believe me. They will all think I have lost my mind. Maybe I have!*

How could a dream-come-true, fantastic chocolate bunny turn into a hairy, fuzzy-tailed rabbit? He couldn't believe it himself.

He ran all the way home to his den. There, he curled up with his mama and papa and he was scared no more.

Chapter 21

The hawk had been scouring for food all morning, floating high above the Carson Valley. His keen eyes kept watching the ground for even the slightest stirring of a rodent. He watched the blades of grass for any movement at all, but he saw nothing. He flew down the mountain range into the foothills and then over the pastures. When the cows were out in the fields, food was scarce. Cows were such huge, lumbering, mooing animals, they scared any hawk's food sources away. If any critters did stay around, there was no way to get to them because their enormous cow bodies blocked any chance of reaching even the slowest field mice.

He flew over the alfalfa fields. Workers and tractors were in those fields, so there would be no mice or critters there today. The hawk soared as high as he could get, then he floated like a feather in the sky; round and round he drifted. He flapped his wings, then drifted again—flap, flap, drift; flap, flap, drift; flap, flap, flap, drift.

He could see for miles. Every once in a while, he would flap his giant wings again, and then float in a circle around the whole valley, never once taking his eyes off the ground. Sometimes he was as high as the glider planes soaring way above the valley. Today, though, there was not a morsel to be seen anywhere. He was hungry.

He had a sudden thought: *I will go back and look for that rabbit now.*

He made a wide turn and headed east, back toward the Pine Nut Mountains. Once again, he flew high above that tan house where he'd found the bunny the day before. He saw some activity there. The humans were packing up the red Jeep with lawn chairs, a cooler, and a wicker basket. Everyone was packing the car, except for the boy.

Silly little boy, he was looking here and there, into and under the bushes and brush. *I'll bet he is still looking for that rabbit,* the hawk thought. *You are wasting your time, little boy. Ha, ha, ha, ha.* The hawk flipped his head back and laughed.

When he got to the Pine Nut Mountains, he knew

that his memory was serving him well as he landed in the exact same tree that he'd sat in the day before. He could usually sit in a tree for hours, just gazing into every nook and cranny of the area, waiting for some unsuspecting creature to come out from under the brush or pop out of a hole. But today he just wanted to know where he'd dropped that boxed rabbit. He looked and he looked, trying to see what bush it might have fallen into. He was sure this was the right spot, but where was the box?

He decided to take flight again, and he circled and circled the area. The sun rose a tiny bit higher, and now its bright rays hit the cellophane on the top of the box. It hit at just the right angle to make it shine like a diamond. It almost blinded the hawk for a second.

"Aha, there it is!" the hawk said with delight. "Just in the nick of time. I am starving."

The hawk was just ready to dive into the bush to retrieve his treasure when a frightening smell hit his tiny nostrils. His feathers stiffened and almost stood on end. Fear gripped his whole body, and his little hawk stomach did somersaults and turned nearly inside out. Almost frozen by fear in midair, it was all he could do to gain control of himself. When fear lost its grip, he zoomed at warp speed back to the top of the tree.

Oh, that smell. Every animal in the world knew and feared that smell. The unforgettable smell of . . . *BEAR!*

The smell of bear was enough to scare even a fearless hawk to death.

Chapter 22

The hawk sat at the top of the tree for the longest time, not moving a feather, barely daring to breathe. Only his eyes moved. They darted back and forth, up and down, looking in every direction for the bear that went with that smell.

There was nothing. He saw nothing; he heard nothing. He waited and watched and listened—still nothing. He waited and waited, but still there was no trace of a bear. After what seemed to be an eternity, he finally decided the bear must be gone, so it would be safe to fly down and grab the box. He waited a bit longer just to be sure, and also to let his still-racing heart slow down to normal speed.

As he waited, he kept his eyes on the box and the furry rabbit inside it. For the first time, he actually got a good look at the whole rabbit. Now he had to rethink where he would eat the bunny. He most definitely could not stay here, where the bear could come back. He couldn't go to the fields, as there were too many workers there. Not the pasture either—it was filled with 200 cows stumbling around. Then he had an idea—the tan house! The very house he had snagged the bunny from in the first place!

The humans would be gone by now, and this house was one of the only houses around that had lots of sagebrush and rabbit brush for cover. Best of all, no one was around to bother him. *Yes!* That was where he would take his prize.

He cast one more look from atop the tree for signs of the bear. He saw nothing, so he decided to dive down like a bolt of lightning, grab the box, and then soar like a jet and get as far away as he could from the smell of bear.

And that's exactly what he did. In a split second, he had the box in his huge talons and off he went. He was going to take no chances this time that the box would get too heavy, so he hung onto it for dear life.

He flew once over the tan house. The Jeep was gone, and no one was in sight for miles. He knew the humans had packed up that morning and were gone—maybe for days. Who knew, and who cared? They were gone for now. The hawk saw the perfect spot—a sagebrush bush that was a bit taller than the rest.

Behind that bush will be the perfect place for this meal, he thought. He could hardly wait to set the rabbit down onto the ground. The hawk was anxious to finally look into the box and get a good look at the tasty rabbit with those huge ears.

Chapter 23

The hawk was so hungry he thought he could almost eat the cellophane window. But no, he did not want to spoil the taste of his delectable cuisine. The only thing keeping him from his rabbit right now was a twisty metal thing wrapped tightly around the top of the cellophane. He tugged and tugged with his perfectly hooked beak. However, his beak was so huge and the wire so tiny that he had to struggle to get hold of it. Finally, though, with one fierce yank and zing, it was gone.

He could see the furry brown rabbit cowering at the bottom of the box, but when he leaned in, he could not quite reach it. He tried getting his talon inside the cellophane, but it did not work. He could not reach that bunny. He poked his head in. The rabbit moved, startling him a bit. The hawk jerked back. He tried again, and this time he caught the rabbit's ear with his beak. He started pulling the rabbit out of the box, thinking, *This rabbit is going to taste terrific! Worth every bit of the wait!*

Just then, somewhere in the world, someone must have seen a rabbit and said, "I believe, I believe," because just as the hawk started taking a big bite of the rabbit's ear, the fluffy, furry, breathing rabbit suddenly turned back into a smooth, silky, sweet chocolate rabbit. The power of that one person saying "I believe" gave the bunny the magical strength to turn back into chocolate.

The hawk spit out the tiny piece of ear. *What is this?* the hawk thought. *Egads, what a horrible taste in my mouth. Yuck, ick. Even as starving as I am, I could never eat anything like this. Not even if I hadn't eaten in a year. Never! Yuck! What just happened?*

He slowly looked into the box. *That's not a rabbit. What is it? No fur, no tail, no movement. It's just a horrible lump of yuck in the shape of a rabbit. Good golly, how can that be? Yikes! And that horrible, sickening, sweet smell.*

The hawk was totally baffled, but he was also starving. The strangest thing in the world just happened, but he still needed to eat. He shook his head and thought, *I'll go find something to eat. I'll come back tomorrow and think about this puzzling situation.*

The hawk had very little daylight left, and he had wasted way too much time on this bunny. What a mystery indeed! All this trouble for one meal, and now it was time to find something else to eat or starve. Even though he was totally baffled at what had just happened, he had no time to figure it out. He only had time to find something else to eat, and he had to do it now or die.

Now that the alfalfa fields looked empty of workers, he would go there and find something to eat. He scratched his head with his long reddish-brown wing and took one more look. *Phooey*, he thought.

He flew away, leaving whatever that brown rabbit-shaped thing was lying motionless by the bushes and in the dirt. It would be sunset soon, so he only had a sliver of time left to catch a meal before dark.

Chapter 24

"Momma! Momma! Over here!" the little fawn called to her mom. "Look, Mom! Come look at what I've found!"

"What is it, dear?" She walked over and stood by her fawn. "Oh. Oh, my," the doe said.

"Is it dead, Momma? Is it dead?"

"Hmm, I don't know, dear. Let me have a closer look."

"Sure is a funny-looking rabbit, Mom. It has no fur!  And look at its ear. There is a hole in its ear, like someone took a bite out of it. Do you think that's what happened, Mom? Do you? Is it dead, Mom? What do you think happened? Is it breathing? Can you see if its heart is beating, Mom? Huh? Can you?"

"Oh, I don't know yet, dear," the doe replied. "Let me get in a little closer."

"Mom, do you—"

"Why don't you walk over there and look for something for us to eat? I'll look and see what's happened to this little peculiar-looking rabbit."

"But, Mom, I found it."

"I know, dear, but let me just have a quiet moment here, while you go and eat something."

"Okay, Mom. You're right. I am hungry." The little fawn took another look at the funny-looking little rabbit shape lying there so still, shook her head, and scampered off.

"Momma," the fawn now called from further away. "I found something else. Mom, I found a box, and it has writing on it. Let me see if I can read it. Yes, the box says, 'The Real Chocolate Rabbit.' What does that mean, Mom? What is chocolate, Mom? Could the bunny have come from this box? Is that a chocolate rabbit?"

"I don't really know, dear. Go on now and find something to eat. I'll stay here."

The doe ever so slowly leaned down to look at the

odd-looking, lifeless rabbit. She looked very closely but could see no beating heart. All the doe could think was that it was indeed one of the strangest looking things she had ever seen. It had no fur, and she could not hear any breathing. *What a peculiar little creature,* she thought. *Are you even a rabbit at all?*

She leaned over still closer to look and nudged the rabbit a bit with her muzzle. Then she gently ran her soft tongue across its still little face.

My goodness. She was surprised and quite delighted at the taste it left in her mouth. The strange little thing was ever so sweet. *What a wonderful flavor,* she thought. *Actually, it's absolutely delicious. I have never tasted anything as delightful as this in my whole life. This sweet rabbit tastes even better than Pat's sweet lavender roses, and those have always been my favorite—until now. This little rabbit must have come from that box. This taste must be the taste of chocolate. This is a chocolate rabbit!*

Just as the doe went back for another lick, the lifeless chocolate creature stirred and, right before her very eyes, something happened that mystified her. In seconds, the sweet, odd-looking chocolate rabbit became a supple, fluffy, furry, real, breathing rabbit. Though it still did not move, she could see its little heart beating. It did not make a sound, but she could see it breathing. And all the sweet chocolate smell was gone. The rabbit had been chocolate one minute and a real living rabbit the next. It was indeed what it said on the box: he was a *Real Chocolate Rabbit.*

The doe was oh so confused about this rabbit, but she knew that no matter what kind of bunny it was, it was very special. She leaned back down and kept licking it ever so softly, hoping that licking it would help bring it around. She was a little bit disappointed that the rabbit did not taste as good as before, but she thought it might help the little rabbit, so she kept licking it.

Her fawn returned from nibbling on a bush. "What is going on, Mom?" she asked. "Is it dead? Is it, Mom? Let me have a look, will ya? Wow, it looks different. It looks like a real rabbit. What happened, Mom?"

"I don't know dear," the doe said. "I don't know what to say about this bunny rabbit."

"Are you sure that's the same rabbit, Mom? Hey, Mom, is it a boy rabbit or is it a girl rabbit, Mom? Huh?"

"I do not know, dear. I just don't know what to tell you."

"Mom, is it okay if I lie down next to this little bunny? It's going to get cold now that the sun is down." The fawn looked down at the little bunny and thought, *Sure looks like a rabbit now. Bet it could use a friend, that's for sure.*

The fawn's mom nodded an okay, so the little fawn dropped down and lay very close to the little rabbit. She gave the little bunny a lick on the ear, the one that had the bite out of it. The fawn then snuggled in as close as she could so they would both be nice and warm. The doe scratched out a little area next to both of them and lay down for the night, still wondering what had just happened with this strange little creature.

Chapter 25

The rabbit lay motionless. Once again, he did not know what was going on. All he knew was that the doe's and the fawn's touch felt so wonderful, and he wanted them to do it again. Just as he thought about their touches, the doe leaned in and gave him a little lick and another tiny nudge with her nose. The bunny, still dazed and with his ear still hurting, just lay there, enjoying her soft nudges and the warmth from the small fawn's body curled up beside him.

The rabbit stayed very still. He felt so beat up, so defeated. Life was one huge danger and full of awful bullies. *Every time you pick yourself up*, he thought, *something or someone punches you back down. Every time something feels good, someone tries to take the good feelings away or, worse yet, they try to eat you.*

The Real Chocolate Rabbit lay there and thought about his short little life so far. He first remembered being on that conveyor belt in the factory, moving toward that horrible sound. *Kaboom, kaboom.* He did not know what the sound was, but he knew it was not good. *Kaboom, kaboom.* It kept getting louder and louder, and the vibrations stronger and stronger. The conveyor belt kept moving him closer and closer to the *kaboom.* The noise was so loud he remembered feeling like he was almost right next to it. *Kaboom, kaboom.*

Then all of a sudden, he remembered being lifted off the conveyor belt and whisked away until he could no longer hear that awful *kaboom* sound. He could not see who had picked him up, but he just knew he felt safe, and that felt good. Then, he remembered being handed over to the boy Artie—what a feeling that had been. It was wonderful.

He remembered Artie squealing with delight as he held him close to his heart, but not so close as to break his ears off. The rabbit, still not moving, thought how warm it made him feel inside for the first time ever to feel affection and kindness from the little boy, Artie.

Love. That's what he was feeling—*love.* He was feeling it again right now with the doe and the fawn lying so close to him. He wanted to feel these good feelings forever.

Chapter 26

The rabbit lay there, delighting in the soft caresses of the doe and fawn. He thought, *This is an incredibly wonderful feeling.* He also realized that in his short life, this was the second act of affection and kindness he had ever known. Once, when the boy Artie held him in the factory, and now again, as the doe and fawn soothed his tired and sore little body. He realized there was indeed more to this life than *kabooms*, hawks, bears, fear, and harm. He liked these new feelings, surrounded by his new friends. These new feelings more than made up for the pain and all the cruelty in the world that the others had brought.

After what seemed like a very, very long time, the little bunny finally shook his head and sat up, still wobbly but alive. Yes, *alive*, really alive. He wasn't a molded chocolate rabbit anymore; he was a real rabbit.

The happy rabbit snuggled back into the folds of

the fawn's legs, where it was warm and safe. As he lay there, the doe started talking. She started explaining a little bit about life to him, life as she knew it. Her sleepy fawn listened also.

"I must say," the doe began, "you are the strangest little critter I have ever met. It is a wonder how one second you could be as sweet as a chocolate candy bar and the next you have fur, a beating heart, and a fluffy tail, like all other rabbits in the world. I know it really does not matter how much I wonder about you, as I am very sure I will never know the answer to the questions I have. Maybe that is not for me to know. It is surely something I will always ponder though."

Chapter 27

The doe continued. "Very possibly, we were brought together tonight so I could pass along a few tidbits of knowledge—things I have learned in my life that might help you with yours. I will try to share these things with you, but it will be up to you to remember what I've said and follow through. You are a very special rabbit. You have special strengths. It will be up to you to try to keep yourself from harm. You are the only one that can.

"You must be very careful out in the world, little one. Remember my words tonight, as we will be leaving you in the morning. We will not come back here tomorrow, and I am sad to say you cannot come with us. We must find a new place to sleep every night. This is something you also will need to do for your own safety. I hope someday you will find a home of your own with incredible little rabbits just like you, but until that day comes, keep my words in mind.

"There will be hawks flying above you that you must watch out for during the day. But keep your eyes on the ground. The shadow the hawks cast makes it easier for you to see them than looking up into the sky. Even the largest hawks look like specks up there because they are flying so high. They are almost impossible for you to see from the earth. But when they are up there one thousand or two thousand feet in the sky, you mustn't forget they can see you as clear as can be. They can see everything on the ground, even the tiniest mouse running through foot-high grass. That's why they say, 'He has the eyes of a hawk.'

"Hawks may indeed have keen eyesight, but they still cannot see under the bushes or big thick brush. These plants are your friends and will provide cover for hiding. The hawks will try to flush you out if they've seen you dive in for cover. They will fly low and strike the top of the bush you are hiding under. They will keep striking, hoping you will get so scared, you will run. But be strong, be still, and wait. Don't let them flush you out into the open. Don't try to run. Never try and run.

"It could be a very, very long wait, but stay still until

you actually see them fly far away. Hawks are lightning fast, and it is impossible to outrun them, so do not try. Their shadows, though, are always a giveaway that they are up there. Do not forget, they are tiny dots if you look up into the sky, but they cast a huge shadow on the ground that you can always see.

"Often, if you listen very carefully, you can hear their call. It almost sounds like a shrill cry in the sky. You'll learn in time how to recognize the various bird sounds, especially the distinct sounds of the different hawks. Most birds mean you no harm—even enormous eagles would prefer to eat fish, but hungry enough, even eagles will come for you.

"Some of the hawks and all the owls in this part of the country will want to eat rabbits.

"The hawks hunt during the daylight hours, but the owls come out to feed at night. There is no shadow at night to see the owls. Your only warning is the whooshing sound of their giant wings. Though sometimes you will hear a cry or a hoot or a squeak. Maybe this

is why God gave you those nice big rabbit ears: all the better to hear the dangers of the world.

"You must keep moving, my little friend. You must never stay in the same place for very long, ever. Coyotes, dogs, even cats have a super keen sense of smell, and they will smell wherever you have been and find you. They can find you just as fast by smell as by sight. You must keep moving and changing where you stay.

"Wherever you go, you leave your scent. If you stay in the same spot too long, animals will be able to pick up that scent. Everything you touch or lie on marks that area with your special odor, so the longer you stay, the stronger your smell will be. A stronger smell makes it easier for those that want to harm you to get a whiff of you."

Chapter 28

The doe continued her lessons on life. "After it rains, you can start all over again in your old place if you want, because the rain carries away odors and smells. Be thankful for the strong winds also, and especially for the afternoon zephyrs. When the winds blow through this valley, they also will help erase your scent, sending it to who knows where. There have been no winds today. That is why we will not stay anywhere near here again tomorrow. If we did, we would be found by something. We will sleep well here tonight, but we must leave you first thing in the morning and move on.

"Be cautious every moment, little one, but do not worry or be frightened all the time. Just be cautious. There will be wonders to see, and many new experiences await you—new sights, sounds, and smells. Enjoy them every day: new things to feel and lots of awesome things to learn. Life is an adventure—your adventure—and yours alone to live. It will be sad at times, scary at times; sometimes it will be just plain unfair.

"You will cry because you have been hurt. You will shriek when you get scared and whimper when you are bullied or picked on. You will weep when life is bad and hurts you. But through those tears, remember there will be tears of joy and happiness when life is good and beautiful. When you have the good in life, these feelings will well up inside you, and there will be no words for how magnificent you feel, just tears of joy flowing.

"You will squeal with laughter when you are happy, and you will have so much fun; there are no words to express the wonder of the moment. You will see that life is a mixture of so many things to feel, but that is for you, little one, to experience on your own. Each day has its own wonder and, without the bad, how could you measure and hold onto the good?

"Do not forget, little bunny, you will never know how great life can be and what wonders it holds if you give up. No matter how bad it gets, hold on to what is good. Try to think about how many magnificent things the future can hold. Remember what I've said, dear little one. Sleep soundly, special little rabbit. You are safe. We are all safe together for tonight."

Chapter 29

The doe and the fawn left the little bunny first thing in the morning. It was not easy for them to leave, but leave they did. For their safety and the safety of their new little friend, they knew there was nothing else they could do.

The rabbit was alone now. He was sad and scared after they left. He was feeling yet another new feeling for him—loneliness. He tried to remember and hold onto the loving feelings he'd had while curled up with the doe and the fawn during the night. It made him feel warm and good inside, but then he would hear a twig crack or see a shadow of some sort and he'd get frightened and run back over to his box. That was where he felt safe again. His box was the only place he felt safe, now that he was on his own.

The bunny kept remembering the doe saying, "Do not stay in the same place; they can pick up your scent.

They will smell you. They will find you. Keep moving on, little rabbit. Each day, keep moving." But the rabbit was so scared when he ventured out. If he thought he saw a shadow, he darted back into his box. He would try again, but every time he thought he heard a screech in the sky, he would dart back to the bottom of his box.

Everything was so new to the rabbit, and his short life had given him no knowledge about anything. He did not know what to be aware of, so he was fearful of everything. He had a lot to learn. When he sat there feeling really terrified, he tried to remember how it felt when the little boy Artie held him close or when he had snuggled with the doe and fawn. When he thought of these things, he felt happy. He wanted more of those happy feelings and less of the bad ones.

He knew he had to move on. He knew that, in order to have more of the good feelings, he had to be strong and take a chance. But move to where? He did not know. How? He did not know. He just knew he needed to go.

Okay. This is it, he thought. *Now is the time. I'll do it!* He tried to move, but he could not. *Oh,* he thought again, *I just want to stay here in the comfort of my box.*

A few minutes later, he thought, *Maybe now, I will just poke my head out and take a look see and go over to that big bush for a moment. Alright, I'll try it right now.*

He started crawling out from the back of his box, when—*Wham*!! He saw them! Huge, red, watering eyes and gigantic, razor-sharp, yellow fangs, all sitting behind wet and snorting nostrils.

A black, runny nose was pushing its way into the cellophane of his box.

Chapter 30

It was a coyote. The doe had warned him about these creatures too.

Oh my gosh, this is it. It's not going to be that hawk, but a coyote that gets me after all. Oh, I'm scared. I don't know what to do. What did the doe say last night? "It's up to you to keep yourself from harm. You are a special rabbit and have special strengths." Can I change? he asked himself. *Can I change myself back? Can I change back into chocolate? Do I even know how?*

I have never tried, he thought. *I wonder if I can do it.* The little rabbit thought. *Maybe I do know how. Maybe I can change right now, from real to chocolate. Do I have the strength? Do I believe I can? Yes, I have the strength. Yes, I believe I can!*

His fur suddenly melted into the same smooth, silky, shiny chocolate from before. He was the same Real Chocolate Rabbit he'd been in the factory, except for the bite out of his ear.

The snarling coyote just snorted and laughed. "Ha," he said out loud. "I'm a coyote, little bunny. I will eat anything. Hmm, actually, I eat everything. I will eat both you and that box for lunch. It does not matter one tiny bit whether you are flesh and bone with fur or a silky-sweet rabbit made of chocolate. It matters little to me which you are. Either way, I will find you yummy and tasty." The coyote's drooling tongue swung loosely from his slimy lips.

Just as the coyote's open muzzle came close enough to grab the chocolate bunny, the sky darkened. It was a shadow. Out of the brilliant blue sky came—the hawk.

The hawk saw that the coyote almost had hold of *his* rabbit. It was *his* box and *his* rabbit. He had so wanted that rabbit for himself; he had worked hard for it for himself. Even though he hated the chocolate smell and had no desire to eat it now, and he still had no clue how that rabbit could be one thing one moment and another the next, there was no way he was going to let that horrid canine animal have *his* rabbit. No way.

The hawk took off like a NASA rocket—up, up, up into the sky. Then, in a flash, he turned around and plunged toward the earth. When he got near enough to the horrible beast, he stuck his enormous talons deep into the coyote's neck.

"Ouch." yelped the coyote. *What the heck was this?*

The coyote reared up on his back legs and tried to shake the hawk off his back, but the hawk was going nowhere. He just dug in a little deeper. They tussled and twisted and turned. Dirt was kicked up, and all the while the little bunny, now once again a living, breathing, petrified-almost-to-death bunny, watched from the back of his box. As the Real Chocolate Rabbit stared in horror as his two enemies writhed and wrangled in the sagebrush, he knew deep inside one of them would prevail.

One of them would come back for him. The only home he'd ever known was no longer safe. In an instant, he made the decision of his life. He worked up all his might and inched to the edge of his box. He looked at his fighting enemies and then, ever so slowly, he crept away. He thought if he was really careful and moved really slowly, they would not notice him in all the commotion.

The wind had come up and blown a big, brown paper bag near a large sagebrush bush nearby, leaving just enough room for the rabbit to crawl under and wait things out. He knew the wind would send his scent far, far away, and he'd be safe here. The doe had told him this, and he believed it.

The hawk and the coyote continued to tangle. The coyote tried to shake the hawk loose again, but the grip of the hawk's massive claws was too great; the coyote was having no luck. The coyote was about to give it his very best burst of energy, when up the dirt road came the red Jeep, heading right for them.

Chapter 31

"Grandpa, Nana, look!" Artie shouted. "What is that?"

"Strangest thing," Grandpa said. "Look at that, Jean. It's a big hawk. He's taken on a coyote. Good grief, I have never in all my days seen such craziness. Look at that, will ya? Golly, have you ever seen such a thing?"

Grandpa Art was amazed, and he kept looking at the hawk and the coyote in disbelief. "Jean," he said, "that ol' coyote is trying his darndest to get away, but that hawk has one mighty strong grip on his neck. Unbelievable."

"Honk the horn a little, Art, and see if that breaks them up," Nana Jean suggested.

Beep, beeeeep. Grandpa Art honked the Jeep's horn.

"Oh, look at that!" Grandpa Art cackled. "Broke 'em up alright. Look at that critter run. I swear, kids. That bird is going after him. Look at that! He is really chasing him. I'll be darned. I have never seen such a crazy thing. Look at them go."

"Grandpa, Jaymee, Nana Jean, look!" Artie shouted again. "Look over there in the bushes! Over there off the road. It looks like the Real Chocolate Rabbit box from the factory, the one we brought to you from home. Oh, we have to go and take a closer look!"

Artie barely waited for the Jeep to come to a stop before he started opening the door.

"Artie, honey, I really don't think that is a good idea," Nana said.

"Why not, Nana?" Artie asked. "It's the best present we ever got for you and Grandpa."

"Artie," Nana said gently. "That box and the chocolate rabbit have been lying out there for a night and a whole day. One can only imagine what's been at it. Artie, there are field mice, skunks, and squirrels, not to mention the hot sun. Do you know what that heat would do to your wonderful chocolate rabbit? Any of those things would not be a pretty sight for you and Jaymee to see. It would be better just to let your grandpa go out with a bag and a shovel. Then you'll always have the memory of that cute rabbit the way he was when you got him."

"Oh no, Nana, I just have to go and see. I really believe it will be okay! Don't you, Jaymee? I really believe he is okay. Come with me." Artie held his hand out to his sister.

Jaymee pulled her hand away quickly and tucked it behind her back and out of his reach. "No way, Artie," she said. "I do not want to see that terrific bunny broken, eaten, melted, or mushed."

Jaymee stepped toward Artie and drew him aside. She put her arms around his shoulders, looked deep into his dark brown eyes, and softly said to him, "Artie, I really do not think you should go over there. Let Grandpa do it. You loved that chocolate rabbit so much, I don't even know how you were able to bring it with us to give to Grandpa and Nana. Artie, it would break your heart to see him nibbled apart or broken into tiny pieces, or—like Nana said—all melted into a chocolate goo-puddle mess." She turned to her grandparents. "Grandpa, Nana, please don't let Artie go out there."

Artie looked up at his sister and said, "Oh, Jaymee, I know you and Nana and Grandpa are just looking out for me, but I really do believe that no harm has come to that chocolate rabbit. I can't explain it,

Jaymee. It's just something I know. Come on. You all have to believe it too."

He reached around and took Jaymee's hand. "Come with me, Jaymee. Just believe, okay? This rabbit has been special from the very beginning at the factory. It'll be fine, Jaymee. Trust me."

Chapter 32

Hand in hand, Artie and Jaymee walked over to where the box lay. Artie bent down and, at first, just looked into the box.

Jaymee squeezed both of her brown eyes shut as tightly as she could and kept them that way until she heard Artie say, "Look, Jaymee; it is empty."

Behind them came their grandpa and nana. Artie reached over and picked the box up. "See?" he said. "No chocolate pieces or parts or melted rabbit at all. But Grandpa, what's this?" Artie held the box up for Grandpa Art to look at.

"Gee, Artie, it looks like rabbit fur. Show it to your Nana Jean. She knows critters much better than I do."

Artie reached in, pulled out the little tuft of fur, and handed it to his grandmother.

"Isn't that something," Nana said. "Wonder how rabbit fur could have gotten into a chocolate box?

Nothing that a rabbit would go in there for. Rabbits eat flowers and greens; they wouldn't ever be interested in chocolate. But that's what it is alright: rabbit fur. Cottontail or jackrabbit for sure, I'd say."

As they walked back to the Jeep. Artie thought the box felt a little heavy, so he reached in and felt under the bottom flap. He felt something pointy in there. When he pulled it out, he could not believe his eyes. "Look! Look at this, everyone!" he squealed.

"What is it, Artie? What did you find?" Jaymee asked.

"It's the star! It's the yellow chocolate star that the Real Chocolate Rabbit had. The star that said 'I believe.' But feel it. This is not chocolate. This star is heavy and looks like gold. Look, everyone."

"Good Lord, child," Nana Jean said. "You surely must have gotten too much sun today. You are not making any sense at all."

"Well, look," Artie said. "Just look for yourselves."

They all stopped walking and circled around Artie, looking at the golden star he held in his little hand.

"Holy cow, Jean. That looks like real gold, doesn't it?"

"Oh, my goodness, Art. Don't be so silly! Now you're

the one not making any sense. That can't possibly be real gold. A star of real gold? Come on, now. You know that would be worth a fortune if it were."

"Let me see that, son," Grandpa Art said.

Grandpa Art took the golden star out of Artie's hand and was shocked to feel how heavy it was. "This is how to test to see if a coin is real gold or just fake fool's gold." He put the star between his teeth and then bit down on it, just exactly the way they always do in the cowboy movies.

"By golly!" Grandpa Art exclaimed, "This feels like the real thing, Artie! Real gold. I don't know how in the world it could be, but sure seems like it to me, kiddo."

"Look, Grandpa, there's more. There's six more in the box."

"I know it's crazy, Artie, but if they are real gold, you and your folks would never have to worry about money again. But let's hold on here until we know for sure. We'll call Rex and Blanche. They own the gold and coin store in town. We'll see if we can go by and have them take a look at these and tell us exactly what's going on. But mark my words, kids, this sure feels like real gold."

Grandpa Art handed the star back to Artie. "The money that gold would fetch would be more than enough to save your house and take care of you and your family forever. Pretty nice college fund for you and Jaymee, too. Yep! Mark my words. Well, let's go to the house so I can make that call."

Chapter 33

No one realized that, just a few feet away, the Real Chocolate Rabbit lay as still as could be under the large brown paper bag. He was petrified as he watched the boy Artie reach down and pick up his box. The rabbit became panic-stricken as Artie carried it away. That box was the only home the Real Chocolate Rabbit had ever known. He knew the box wasn't safe anymore, but just knowing it was there had given him comfort. He had been slipped into it at the factory, and he had never ever been very far away from it all his life.

The Real Chocolate Rabbit was more fearful right now than when he had been facing the coyote's ginormous fangs or that humongous hawk. The little rabbit had no place to go, no place to hide, no friends, and now no box for a home. No place at all to call his own; just this brown paper bag on top of his head—though he was indeed very grateful for that much protection!

The wind started picking up and getting stronger by the minute. The rabbit was so terrified, he thought, *This just isn't worth it. Life is too hard.* His little heart began beating as fast as a hummingbird's wings. It was beating in his chest so fast it was making him feel weak and woozy. He could hardly breathe. *Now I do not even have a box to go to. I have no place to hide. I have no place to go*, he thought.

Somewhere deep down inside his heart, he knew that Artie had just saved his life by taking the box away. He knew that he would have climbed right back into the box when everyone was gone, and then either the hawk or the coyote would be back to get him.

But his head was saying, *I thought that Artie was my friend. I thought he liked me. Why did he take my box? What am I to do now? The hawk or the coyote or even a bear will come back and pick on me again; almost everyone picks on me. One of them is going to come and they will get me. What am I going to do?*

Then he got the answer.

NOTHING. *I'll do nothing. I will stay here and do nothing. I will let the hawk swoop down and grab me, or the coyote can come back and eat me. Then it will be over.*

His box was gone. That was the last straw.

The Real Chocolate Rabbit was done. He quit. He lay on the ground. He was too weak to move, so he stayed under the bag. He felt the wind rustle the bag a little bit, and he felt the bag lift just a little more. He tried to pick his head up to look around, but he could not. He could barely open his eyes. He would just stay here under this bag until one of them returned; or he would just wait for his racing heart to take its last beat.

Then it happened. The wind blew again, this time hard enough to swirl the bag. Up it went and flew far, far away from the little bunny. The Real Chocolate Rabbit just lay there—stretched out, weak, and now with no protection at all. He did not even have the strength or desire to crawl and hide under the bush that was just a few inches away. He was defeated and tired of this unfair life.

Chapter 34

The Real Chocolate Rabbit looked up and into the sky—way, way up, almost in the clouds. There it was: the hawk. Though the little rabbit was so exhausted and weak he could hardly keep his eyes open, for just a second, he thought the hawk's eyes met his. He looked away, pretending it never happened. But when he peeked up again, he knew at once. Indeed, the hawk had seen him. He was coming for him. It was going to be the hawk, not the coyote, after all.

The Real Chocolate Rabbit did not care anymore; he was done. Life was so hard. There were so many dangers, so much to learn, so many bullies. Why go on? Life wasn't fair; it was always knocking you down at every corner. He closed his little eyes and waited. He knew it would only take the hawk a few minutes to reach him. So he lay very still and waited for the hawk to swoop down and get him.

Then the rabbit heard something. It was distant, but it felt close. It was the voice of the boy, Artie. He could hear the boy crying out, "Chocolate rabbit, I believe! Chocolate rabbit, I believe! I know you are out there, and I believe in you!"

He heard Artie say to Jaymee, Nana Jean, and Grandpa Art, "Come on, everyone. The rabbit is out there, and he needs our help. Let him know we believe. Say it, everyone!"

All four looked out into the field and said, "I believe, I believe. We all believe, little rabbit, we all believe!!"

From the porch, everyone could see the hawk plunging through the sky. They all knew he'd seen something and was diving for it. Artie's eyes darted from bush to bush, but he saw nothing. He looked up into the sky. The hawk was still coming. His gaze went back out into the field, looking for any sign of his rabbit.

There! Over there, where the brown paper bag had been! There he is! Artie just knew it was the Real Chocolate Rabbit. Artie stood perfectly still. He did not even dare to blink for fear his eyes would lose sight of the petrified little bunny. Then it happened. The rabbit, lying so still on the ground as if he'd completely given up, lifted his weary little head just the tiniest bit, then tilted it ever so slightly. The rabbit's eyes opened, and the little guy looked right at Artie, even though they were yards apart. Their eyes met and instantly locked.

Artie repeated ever so gently, over and over and over again, "I believe, I believe!" Each time he said it, his voice got a little bit louder and then louder. All of a sudden, everyone on the porch joined in. "I believe, I believe!" Over and over again, they all said, "I believe!"

Then Artie yelled, "Get up! Get up, little rabbit! Please don't quit, little guy. Do not give up; life is worth living! There's lots of living for you. Please *do not* give up. Don't let the bullies in life take you away from the wonderful things of the future. Get up and run . . . Get up and run now!!!!"

Chapter 35

As the rabbit lay there, he started remembering things. He recalled being saved from the crusher at the factory. He remembered how fantastic it felt to be picked up and taken away from the horrible *kabooms*. He remembered how happy he'd felt when the boy Artie held him. Artie was so kind; that thought made the rabbit feel amazing inside. He remembered the joy in Artie's eyes when Leon handed him over. He remembered how terrific it had made him feel when Artie took him out of the bag and showed him to everyone on the airplane. Oh, what delightful feelings.

Then he remembered how it felt curled up with the doe and her fawn—that was comfort and love. Right now, all those good feelings seemed so much more important than all the fear and loneliness he'd been feeling lately. He thought, *Why should I give up and never know more of the happiness in the world? That's what I want in my life. That's what I am going to choose for my life—more of those fantastic feelings. Lots of them; all of them!*

He wondered at that moment what other wonderful feelings were out there to feel. What delightful adventures were out there to do? What were his wishes? What were his dreams? What did this fantastic thing called life have in store for him? These were feelings and experiences he would never get to feel or do if he just gave up and quit now.

He needed to find the strength to get up so he could go after all those magnificent things. He knew there would always be some unhappy moments in his future. There would be some fear, and there would be times he'd be scared and times he'd be bullied. There would be illness and pain, even some confusing and lonely times. But he would spend his life looking for new and amazing experiences—good experiences, happy experiences, and lots of them.

So many things awaited him. Both good and bad. He wanted to know it all, feel it all, live it all. The Real Chocolate Rabbit felt Artie's belief, everyone's belief, and the strength that came with all that belief. Even though belief was something you could not see or touch, he felt it inside. This was a new feeling. He had faith.

As he lay there gazing at Artie, his mind raced with all these new thoughts. The Real Chocolate Rabbit suddenly felt a warm, soft, but steady breeze blow over his body. He closed his eyes so he could concentrate on this new feeling. As the breeze gently tickled his fur, he opened his eyes and looked around. He saw everything else was perfectly still. Not a blade of grass or a leaf on a bush was moving, just his own fur rippling ever so gently.

He started feeling stronger and realized then that this was the feeling of strength—the strength coming from everyone everywhere in the world believing in him. Believing in all Real Chocolate Rabbits everywhere. He lay there and thought, *If they can believe in me, I need to believe in me. They do believe in me. I do believe in me! I do! I can feel the strength welling up inside me.*

He could not understand what was happening, but it felt so good. His foot twitched, and then his paw twitched, and then, just like magic, his whole body felt strong, and he felt ready to go. He realized then that it was the strength that came from within himself that would make him the strongest. He needed to keep believing in himself. The little rabbit felt so good he forgot about the hawk until it was almost too late. He looked up, and the hawk was coming straight for him!

Chapter 36

The hawk zoomed toward the rabbit with his talons spread wide and his beak half open. Within inches of reaching the rabbit, the hawk felt the strong afternoon zephyrs that swept east down the Sierra Nevada mountain range make an abrupt about-face and start blowing west and back up the Sierra mountains. The winds spun the hawk completely out of control. Around and around he spun. And then—*bam!*—he crashed into a giant cottonwood tree, almost knocking his head off. He lay on the ground, dazed from the blow. He could not move, not even a tiny feather. That same wind then stretched out like a giant hand, and it reached down and scooped up the little rabbit, lifting him off the ground and whisking him toward the open range of the Carson Valley.

Oh, what a wonderful new feeling the little rabbit had—the warm, robust, rushing air blowing all around him. He could feel it flowing through his fur; his ears were flopping every which way. His nose was picking up smells he had never smelled before, and his eyes saw the whole valley as never before. He was flying just as the hawk flew, only much lower to the ground.

Then, when the hand of the wind ever so lightly set him back on the ground, the rabbit's little legs kept right on going. Faster and faster his legs went. This, too, was a brand-new experience. Running!

It was freedom! He loved this running thing. He ran and ran as fast as the wind itself for ever so long. What an awesome feeling it was. *Oh, this is one of the most terrific joys of life,* he thought. Oh, he loved these great new things. *Life, yes, it is worth living. It is marvelous.* He was so, so glad he hadn't just given up and quit. He was also very glad the hawk had not eaten him.

When he finally stopped running, he sat on a little hill under a bush. As he gazed out into the majestic Carson Valley, he realized he'd actually had thoughts in his head for the very first time ever. He'd run with the wind for the first time ever. All of this gave him brand-new feelings—happiness, excitement, and a tiny bit of fear, but life seemed worth it, and he liked it.

He sat and he wondered, as he gazed at the

mountains, what other magnificent experiences he would get to know. Were there other rabbits like him? If so, where were they living and what were they doing? What would this gift of life bring? And what would he be able to give back?

THE BEGINNING
for
The Real Chocolate Rabbit

In the Jeep on their way to the coin shop, as they sat at a red light, Artie looked out the window and saw some bushes rustling. Under the bush was a rabbit. Then he saw a shadow hover over the area. He looked up at the sky and saw a hawk. As he watched, he saw the hawk swoop down for a better look into the sagebrush. The bush moved again as the hawk took another run at it.

Artie squealed, "Look, it's a rabbit. Maybe it is another Real Chocolate Rabbit. Nana, Jaymee, Grandpa, quick! Everyone say 'I believe.' Hurry, I know the hawk sees him too. We have to make him strong. Say it, everyone!!"

All at the same time, they said, "I believe, I believe."

Unable to flush the rabbit out, the hawk gave up and flew away.

Artie smiled then reached into his pocket and started jingling his seven gold stars. Then he smiled again and thanked the Lord for his answered prayers.

The End

Life can be upside down, hurtful, or you may just feel lost.
But with a blink of an eye, things can change.
Life can become . . . awesome.

Wait for those magical days;
they are worth it!